About Us

Modern entertainment companies refuse to put their characters to rest, and it causes a feeling of low stakes, or it butchers someone you loved. OHAB Comics seeks to change that. Fed up with an industry that regurgitates characters and storylines over and over again, Shawn Allen and Connor Brown have created a universe in which even the most beloved characters will have a canonical death and never come back, be it through time travel, cloning, multiverses, or technology and the occult. It makes every character, death, and storyline much more meaningful when each character's actions have consequences...

IT IS TIME LOYAL SUBJECT
COME TO ME
MY STAY HERE IS NEARING ITS END

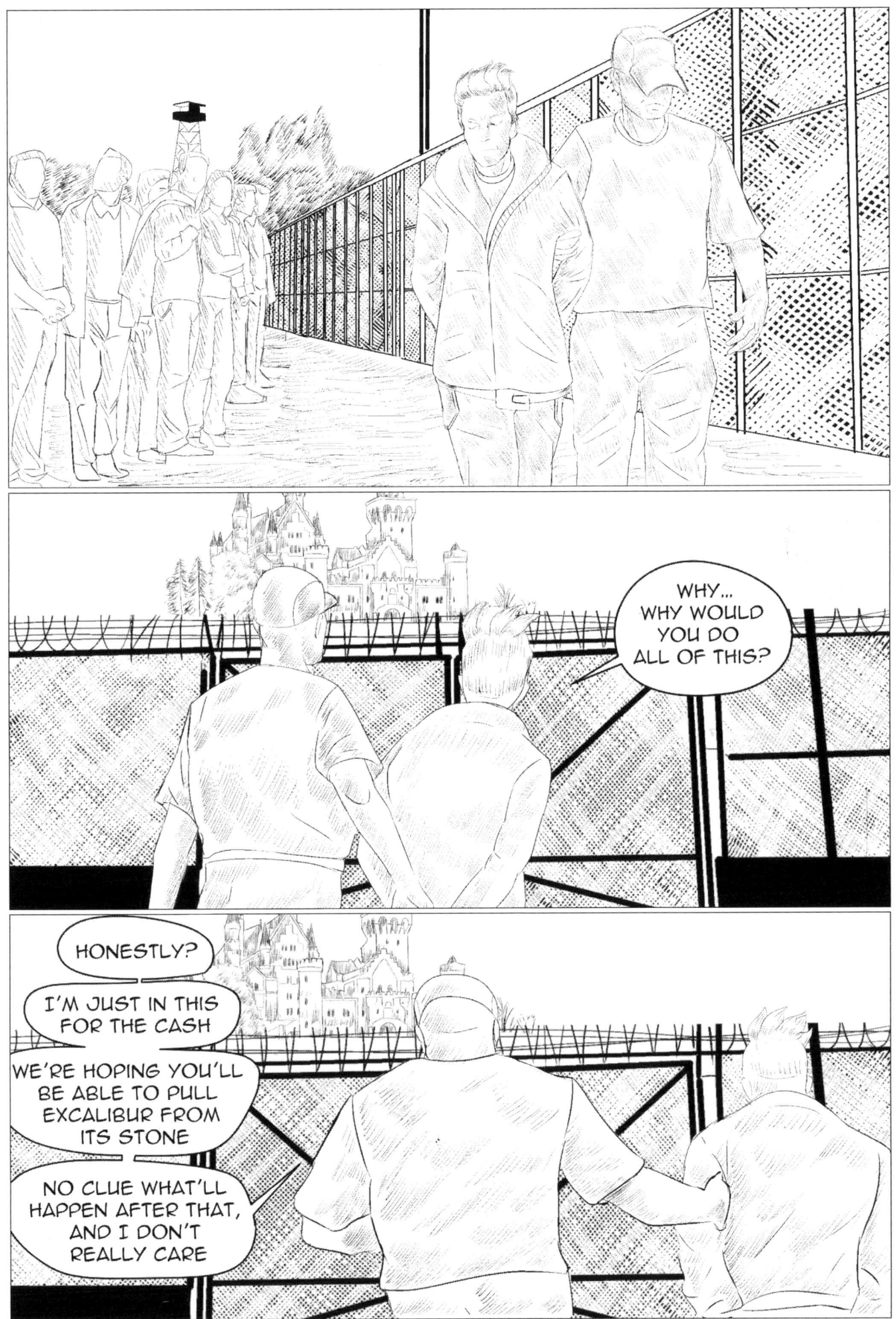

TO BE CONTINUED...